My Garden

Krysia Kij

Rosen REAL READERS

Rosen Classroom Books & Materials
New York

1

This is my garden.

I grow flowers in my garden.

I grow pumpkins in my garden.

I grow peas in my garden.

The sun helps my garden grow.

Rain helps my garden grow.

Words to Know

flowers

garden

peas

pumpkins

rain

sun